Middlebury
P.O. Box 26
432 S. Main St.
Middlebury, IN 46540

W9-BMW-764

Mercer Mayer's
A Monster Followed Me to School

To Frank and Kathy Skiles,
another monster just for you

Mercer Mayer's
A Monster Followed Me to School

A GOLDEN BOOK • NEW YORK
Western Publishing Company, Inc., Racine, Wisconsin 53404

© 1991 Mercer Mayer. All rights reserved. Printed in the U.S.A. No part of this book may be reproduced or copied in any form without written permission from the publisher. All trademarks are the property of Western Publishing Company, Inc. Library of Congress Catalog Card Number: 91-71139 ISBN: 0-307-11466-X/ISBN: 0-307-61466-2 (lib. bdg.)
A   MCMXCI

There was a monster on our block. One day he was just there. I know because I saw him on my way home from school. I was scared that first time, so I ran away.

Before dinner I told my dad. But a monster on our block didn't seem to bother my dad at all. He just smiled and patted me on the head.

Later on, he said I should spend more time figuring out how to do well at school and less time on monsters.

I asked if I could be excused from the table.

After dinner I told my mom. She said it was probably the same monster that used to live under my bed.

I told her this monster looked a lot different.
My mom asked me to explain, but I went to my
room to put on my pajamas instead.

The next day I started walking to school like always. But pretty soon I had a funny feeling that my monster might be following me. He was.

He looked hungry. I didn't want to hang
around with him if he was hungry. I figured he
might do something weird all of a sudden. So I
got out my lunch and gave it to him.

He ate the whole thing, bag and all. Then he burped.

Then he looked right at me and smiled. I
mean he really smiled. That's when I decided he
liked me.

I had to get going, so I started walking again. My monster walked right behind me, but nobody seemed to notice. Not one person said anything, not even the postman.

When I got to school, Biff was waiting for me. He's the school bully. Biff has been pushing me around ever since I was a little kid.

Biff walked up to me. All of a sudden my monster happened to swing his tail around. Biff's legs flew right out from under him. He fell down, and everyone laughed.

Biff thought I did it. He was pretty mad. He told me I was going to get it after school.

I opened my knapsack and got out the book
I'd borrowed from Amy Frobish. But my monster
grabbed the book right out of my hand and tried
to eat it.

When I gave Amy her book, she said she was
going to show it to the teacher.

I'm always getting in trouble.

At school, my monster climbed right on top of the teacher's desk. Then he lay there making faces and sticking out his tongue.

Boy, oh, boy, I thought. Would he ever get in trouble if the teacher saw him doing that. She would tell him he'd better be careful. His face could freeze that way.

Thinking of that made me laugh, which
meant I got in trouble. I had to write I WILL BE
QUIET IN CLASS twenty-five times on the
blackboard.

My monster got tired of waiting for me, so he blew all the papers off the teacher's desk.

She rushed over to close the window. But the window wasn't open.

At recess my monster spent a lot of time on
the slide. He even took turns.

I thought that was great.

Then he played kickball for a while. The best part was when he tripped Biff. Of course, Biff was sure I did it. Boy was he mad. "You're really going to get it!" he yelled.

We were supposed to watch a video called
Birds of Brazil, but the teacher couldn't find it.
My monster was getting hungry again. I think he
ate the video.

We didn't do our work sheets because the teacher couldn't find those, either. My monster probably ate those, too. We drew pictures instead. I drew a picture of my monster. Everyone thought it was dumb.

Then we practiced the song my teacher wrote for Parent's Night. This is how it started:

"When I give my everything,

I have a happy song to sing."

I'm not too crazy about the song.

My monster didn't want to be left out, so he sang along. He didn't really sing. He howled, and it sounded terrible. The teacher kept looking in our direction. I think she couldn't figure out what was going on.

I didn't sing very well, either. If my monster and I sang together a lot, all the kids in my class would probably move away.

After singing practice, my monster left the room. I think he was bored. Or hungry.

The next time I saw him was at lunch in the cafeteria. He waved at me. Then he reached into a big pot of chicken à la king and licked his paw. That was okay with me. I hate chicken à la king.

I bought myself a bag of potato chips. I had to get something because my monster had eaten my lunch.

31

I'm pretty sure our principal saw him later
that day. I was just standing there. The principal
went running down the hall, moaning.

They said he went home after that.

In the afternoon, Amy Frobish showed her beat-up book to the teacher. The teacher made me stay after the bell and write

I WILL TAKE GOOD CARE

OF THINGS I BORROW

twenty-five times on the blackboard.

Then I had to erase the whole blackboard before the teacher would let me leave.

When I finally got out of school, Biff was waiting for me. He was going to beat me up. Everyone was there to watch what happened, even Amy Frobish. First I thought I would run back inside of the school building and hide, but I'd just have to come out sooner or later. Then I thought maybe I should just faint and lie on the ground real still. But then everyone would say I was chicken. No, I decided, I'd just have to get beat up. Then the strangest thing happened.

Biff looked in my direction, and his eyes got big. His mouth dropped open. Then he ran off down the street.

I turned around. There was my monster, right behind me. I guess Biff could see him, too.

What a great feeling. The two of us were too much for Biff.

I started home. I knew my monster was behind me. I figured he'd walk the whole way with me.

When the light turned green, I crossed the street like I always do. But my monster didn't cross behind me. He stayed on the other side, near school.

I watched for a while to see what he was going to do. What he did was turn around and walk back to the school building.

I figured he liked school. Or maybe it was the cafeteria.

BUS STOP

When I got home, I told my mom what
happened. She said school was a good place for a
monster. She liked the part about the principal
running down the hall.

When my dad got home, I didn't tell him what happened. I didn't think he'd like the part about me writing things twenty-five times.

One thing was sure. I was never going to borrow anything from Amy Frobish ever again.

Before it got completely dark, I went outside. I rode my bike around the block just to double-check. My monster wasn't anywhere. We definitely don't have a monster on our block anymore.

He's at my school. I think he lives in the basement there, because this winter the boiler has broken down three times so far. Our janitor always makes his assistant go down there, and our principal quit. They told us he had a medical problem, but I don't think so.

Biff doesn't hit me anymore. He even crosses the street when he sees me coming, which is great. I hope he keeps it up.

I'm even friends with Amy Frobish again.

I'm glad the monster followed me to school. I miss him sometimes. I might want to try to find him again, someday. If I do...

...I can always go down to the school basement and check behind the boiler.